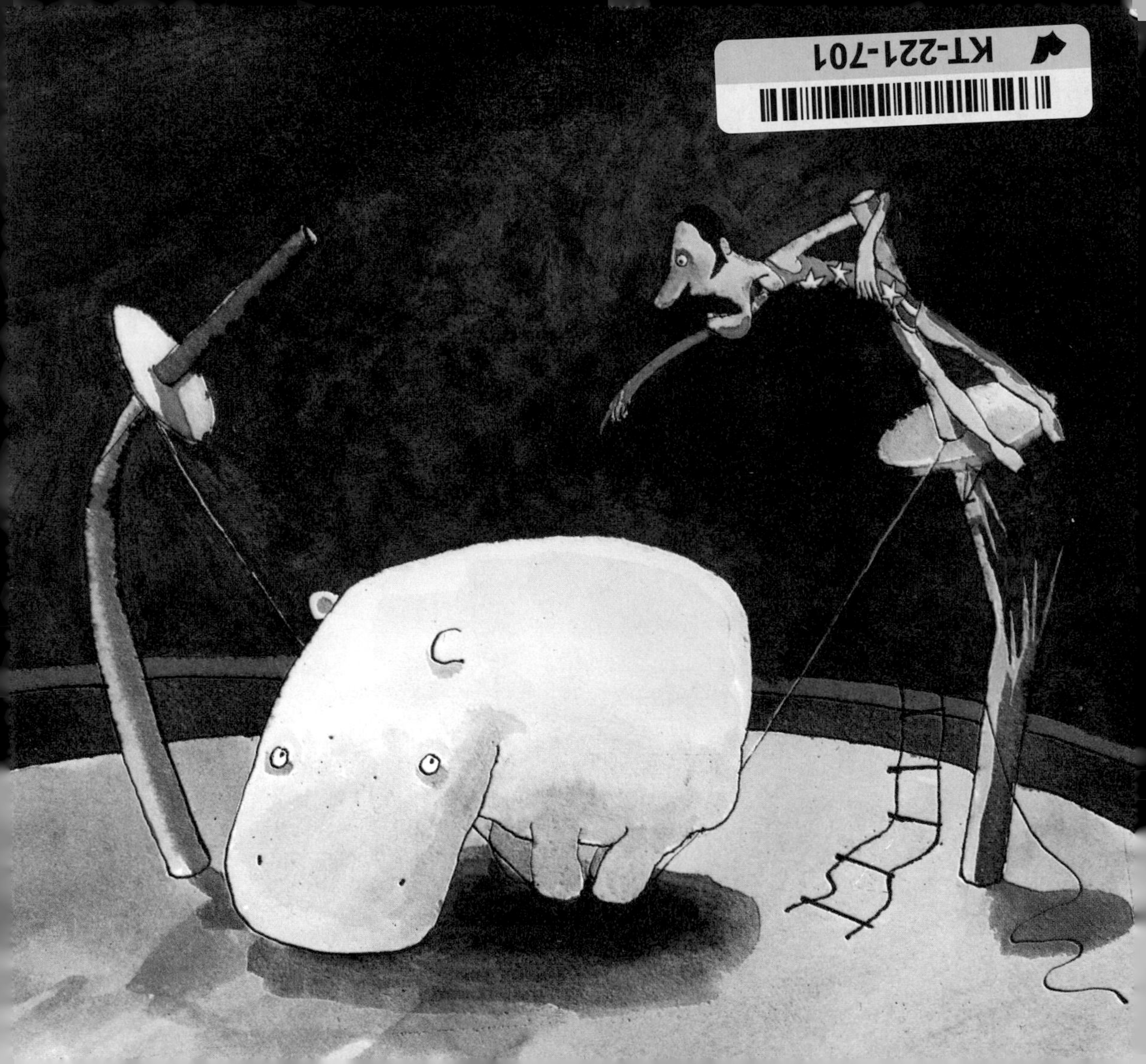

'Oh dear,' she thought, 'I do want to perform in the circus.'
When she stopped running, she spied the big ball which belonged to Ben the performing dog. Ben would walk around the ring on the ball and everybody thought that was pretty clever.
'I'll give it a try,' muttered Big Ethel to herself, and she climbed up on to the ball.
BANG! The noise of the ball bursting roused Ben who was having a nap nearby.
'You silly great lump!' screeched Ben, staring at the remains of his ball. 'Go away before I forget I'm a gentleman and bite you!'
Again Big Ethel took to her heels.
'And stay away!' Ben yelled after her.

It happened that the circus was visiting a seaside town. As no one seemed to appreciate Ethel's efforts to become a star, she wandered away along the beach, lonely and a little sad.

Big Ethel was used to being told to go away . . .

There was that time when she tried to swing on the trapeze and pulled the circus tent down.

And the time she stood on one of Itchy Joe's fleas. The flea was so ill he was in bed for a week. Itchy Joe made such a FUSS!

Ethel mooched along the sand, past the pier, to the rock pools, her favourite spot. She liked to paddle and tell jokes to amuse the crabs.

'HELP, HELP! Oh deary me, HELP!'
Ethel stopped and listened. Searching around, she saw a blob of black gooey stuff with a beak sticking out. The blob was flapping about in a shallow pool.
Gingerly peering at the blob, Big Ethel made out the shape of a bird covered in thick, black oil.
'Thank goodness!' screeched the blob. 'Get me out of here.'
Big Ethel picked up the bird. 'What's the matter?' she enquired.
'WHAT'S THE MATTER!' gurgled the blob. 'Can't you see I'm covered in oil? I'm a sick bird, get me to a vet, quickly!'
Ethel obediently trotted away towards the town.

A policeman showed Ethel the way to the vet and by lunchtime, the blob (who turned out to be a seagull called Norman) was sitting happily in a bath of Oily Bird Cleaner. The vet was scrubbing Norman's back and the gull was in a far better temper.
'Such a nuisance, this oil,' announced Norman.
'It comes from boats out at sea. Once us birds get covered in it, we can't move. We can't fly, we can't feed ourselves, in fact, a lot of us die!'
'Dreadful, dreadful,' chorused Big Ethel and the vet together.
At last, Norman was white and clean again and everybody sat down for a spot of lunch.

When Norman felt stronger, he and Big Ethel said goodbye and thank you to the vet and set off back to the beach.
Big Ethel climbed on to a rock and tossed Norman into the air.
'I can't thank you enough!' called Norman, gliding away.
'Any time I can help ' answered Ethel, waving a hoof.
It was getting late and Big Ethel looked around her in alarm. The tide was coming in fast and the water was rushing round the rock that Ethel was standing on.
Rocks poked out of the swirling water here and there, and the beach looked a long way away.
Ethel began to panic.

The frightened hippo cried 'Oh, oh, oooooooh!' and began to wobble on her rock. With a terrific splash Big Ethel toppled back into the water.
The green sea closed over her and she sank in a cloud of bubbles.
Curious fish rushed up as Ethel was the first hippo many of them had ever seen.
'You really shouldn't be down here,' scolded a cod sternly. 'You can't breathe!'
'GLUG!' answered Big Ethel.
Up swam a helpful plaice, dragging an aqualung kept specially for visitors. 'You'd better put this on while you get back to land,' she advised.

Meanwhile, Norman was gliding about looking for a fish to eat, when he saw a mackerel peeping out of the water. With a swoop Norman had him in his beak.
'STOP!' yelled the mackerel. 'LISTEN!'
He told Norman about the sunken hippo.
'She's quite safe for now,' finished the mackerel, 'us fishes have tried to move her, but she's far too heavy.'
'Well look,' said Norman, 'that hippo's a friend of mine, I won't eat you if you'll do as I say.'
'Yes, yes!' agreed the mackerel.
Norman whispered in the fish's ear and dropped him back into the sea.

The mackerel swam back to Big Ethel who was by that time feeling quite miserable. Not to mention wet!
'Cheer up,' soothed the mackerel, 'everything's taken care of.'
Suddenly, dozens of strings floated down through the water. Ethel couldn't think what was happening, so she just sat there as the fish darted around her tying knots. The strings were fixed tightly to Ethel's nose, her legs and right around her tummy.
When all that was done the strings went tight, and slowly Big Ethel began to rise towards the surface.
'Bye!' sang the fish, waving their fins.

Up, and up, and up went Ethel. When she reached the surface she saw a marvellous sight. Above her, holding on to the strings, were lots of birds. Herring gulls, black-headed gulls, oyster catchers, terns, kittiwakes and a puffin. Norman had brought all his friends.

'Lift a little, terns! Pull harder your end, puffin!' shouted Norman, giving all the orders.

Away they flew with Ethel hanging underneath. Over the beach and the town, towards the circus.

Big Ethel quite enjoyed the flight. She settled back on the strings and enjoyed the scenery. Soon the circus tents loomed into view.

Everybody ran towards Big Ethel and HOW they had changed. 'Thank goodness you're back!' was the cry. Mr. Toffy hugged her, Tiger Harry shook her hoof. You see, although Ethel was sometimes annoying, everybody now knew how much they loved her.
Mr. Toffy thanked the sea-birds for their help and Norman told the whole adventure to the circus folk. Ethel was quite a heroine. She signed autographs and answered questions. For the first time in her life, people WANTED to be with her. Big Ethel was so happy.
'Here's my new ball,' said Ben, 'you may burst it if you like!'
Ethel thanked him.
BANG.